Praise for Amazing Esme

'A hugely enjoyable book . . . young readers will love the imaginative adventures' – *The Bookseller*

'A charming debut' – *Sussex Life*

'Hugely entertaining, and carried along by illustrations that are full of life and fun' – *Carousel*

'This is an incredibly lively book enhanced by copious illustrations . . . highly recommended for reading aloud or for the emerging reader' – *The School Librarian*

'This short novel is ideal both for reading aloud and for newly confident readers to try for themselves. With so many delicious elements to relate to – animals of all kinds, freedom to have adventures and extraordinary circus skills – this fast paced and entertaining narrative will be much enjoyed' – *Books for Keeps*

GASP

AT THE **WONDROUS** UNICORNED PIG.

WITNESS THE **AMAZING** DIVING WEASLES.

MARVEL AT THE PIROUETTING DONKEY.

LAUGH YOURSELF **SILLY** AT A BAD MANNERED TEA PARTY

★ ★ ★ A FOOD-FLINGING **EXTRAVAGANZA.**

BEST OF ALL, MEET THE **STAR** OF THE SHOW –

THE ONE & ONLY

THE AMAZING

ESME

Tamara Macfarlane

Illustrated by
Michael Fowkes

HODDER CHILDREN'S BOOKS

First published in Great Britain in 2011 by Hodder Children's Books
This edition published in 2016 by Hodder and Stoughton

13

A CIP catalogue record for this book
is available from the British Library.

ISBN 978 0 340 99993 6

Printed and bound in Great Britain
by Clays Ltd, Elcograf S.p.A.

The paper and board used in this book
are made from wood from responsible sources

Hodder Children's Books
An imprint of
Hachette Children's Group
Part of Hodder and Stoughton
Carmelite House
50 Victoria Embankment
London EC4Y 0DZ

An Hachette UK Company
www.hachette.co.uk

www.hachettechildrens.co.uk

For Lily, Xander, Steve,

Nell and King

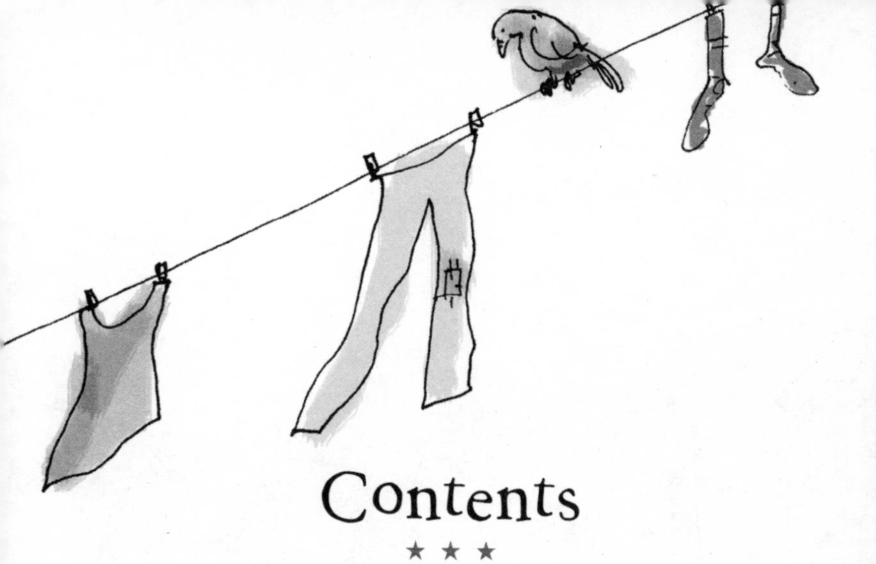

Contents

★ ★ ★

MUNGO MACLINKEY

ESTHER BALFOUR

AUBREY MACLINKEY (UNCLE MAC)

ANGELICA LONGBEACH

HENRY MACLINKEY

CARLOTTA MIRANDA

MAGNUS MACLINKEY

COSMO MACLINKEY

GUS MACLINKEY

ESME

MIRANDA-MACLINKEY

Introduction

★ ★ ★

Maclinkey Castle was so remote that Esme had to be delivered by postal van along with the week's letters and parcels. As she hopped out, grabbed her case and thanked the postman, Esme shook out her brightly-sequinned skirt. She straightened her cowgirl hat on top of her unruly curls and turned her sparkling eyes up to the turrets of the castle.

'Oh my juggling uncles. That is enormous!' she declared, searching the high walls for a way in. She was quite used to climbing, having grown up in the circus, but she wasn't really sure that somersaulting over the wall was the best way to introduce herself to her cousins.

Esme was about to pick up her suitcase when a drawbridge banged down in front of her and a mass of creatures tumbled out, head over heels. Wide-eyed with astonishment, Esme was almost run over by the most extraordinary collection of wildlife that she had ever seen. Clusters of guinea pigs surfed on crocodiles' backs, monkeys steered swans with reins, mice swooped down from the castle walls, perched between the wings of seagulls.

As the animals engulfed her in a welcoming embrace of licks, nudges, squawks and squeaks, a cuddly-looking lady appeared

and flung her arms around Esme, sweeping her off her feet.

ONE

★ ★ ★

The Bad-Mannered Tea Party

'Come along inside, dear,' said Mrs Larder as she shooed a few birds and a monkey out of her way and stepped over a small bear. Esme grabbed her case and followed her over the drawbridge and into the castle hall. They ducked down a narrow set of stairs that opened out into a large room where a feast of the most delicious food imaginable was laid out on an enormous wooden table.

'Have a seat by the fire, ducks. I will

fetch the boys,' Mrs Larder said, picking up an old-fashioned megaphone. Then, climbing onto a box, she stuck her head out of the window. 'Teeeeeeeeeeeea Tiiiiiiiiiiiiiiiiime!' she yelled.

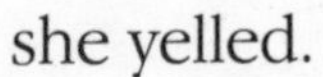

Mrs Larder was the castle housekeeper. She had been looking after Esme's cousins since they were babies. Their father – Aubrey Maclinkey – Esme's Uncle Mac, travelled the world rescuing endangered and mistreated animals and sending them back to Maclinkey Castle for safety. This had caused their mother, Esme's Aunt Angelica, to lose her temper. She had had enough of tipping porcupines out of her bed and clearing perching anteaters from the loo seat, and had moved to New York. She wrote to her boys often and loved them dearly from afar.

As two boys came racing through the doorway, a third tumbled head-first through a window. Esme giggled and smiled warmly.

'Esme, these are your cousins. Magnus,

Cosmo and Gus, this is Esme,' introduced Mrs Larder. Esme was a bit preoccupied, however, staring longingly at the shining bowls of melted chocolate, the plates of scones piled high with cream and jam, the mountains of doughnuts and the tall glass filled to the brim with multi-coloured sweets which threatened to cascade onto the floor.

'Hi, Esme,' said Magnus, patting a passing warthog and scooping up a turtle to examine at the table. The turtle looked up at him lovingly.

'I'm Gus. Can we eat? Can we eat? Can we eat?' chanted the smallest one.

'Oh, you're Esme,' said Cosmo, looking at Esme suspiciously. Then he turned and addressed Mrs Larder. 'Can we have a bad-mannered tea party because Esme is here?'

'Really, Cosmo, you will find any excuse for a bad-mannered tea party!' said Mrs Larder, her voice trailing behind her as she banged through the kitchen door to fetch more food.

The boys took that as a yes and leapt towards the table. Cosmo plunged his hands into the plate of doughnuts and threw two straight at Esme. The first one hit her on the side of her head. Jam oozed into her ear and down her chin. Without even wiping it off, she dived into a multi-coloured bowl of jelly, squooshed out a giant handful and hurled it back. A third doughnut fired by Cosmo skimmed Esme's cheek and landed on the

goat sitting beside her at the table. The goat stuck its hooves into the plate of scones and flicked cream across the table all over an already jelly-covered Cosmo.

A unicorned pig waited by the fireside as a pelican popped marshmallows onto its horn to be roasted. As soon as they were gooey and brown, the pig trotted off around the table to deliver the warm mallows to the children. Gus pulled two sticky gloops off and stuck them into the melted bowl of chocolate. He stuffed them quickly into his mouth at the same time as shouting at Magnus to throw him some sausages. The marshmallows shot straight back out of his mouth and into Cosmo's lap. Gus collapsed in a fit of giggles.

'Gus, that's not just bad mannered, it's really, really disgusting!' yelled Cosmo as he crawled through bowls and plates to smear cake into Gus's hair.

'More mallows, more mallows!' shouted Gus every few minutes. He was covered in chocolate cake and bits of hot cross bun that

Magnus was firing at him.

Cosmo stole the last doughnut from Magnus' plate and disappeared back under the table, hurling things up at Esme as he went.

Esme used all her circus acrobatics skills to dodge doughnuts and dive under jam tarts. She skilfully back-flipped down the table to

escape a dozen sausage rolls. *This is not so different from home*, she thought, remembering breakfast with the clowns in her caravan that very morning.

'That's amazing, Esme!' Magnus paused and watched Esme's acrobatics in astonishment.

'Cosmo, Gus, look at Esme!'

'I'm not looking at anything,' Cosmo called as he bowled another three buttered teacakes along the table at Magnus.

'I can do it too, I can do it too.' Little Gus tried to turn a somersault and ended up with his head in the custard layer of a large bowl of trifle.

Magnus pulled him out and the children threw and shouted, grabbed and feasted with not a please or thank you to be heard until every bowl had been emptied and every plate had been licked clean.

'Come on, Esme,' called Magnus, as he grabbed the last marshmallow from the unicorned pig and stuck it in his mouth.

'Time to show you around.'

Map
For
ESMe
Mrs Larder's room
on other side
play room
otherside
Magnus's room
Gus's
room
Not here
when
he's at
sea!
Maclinkey
Castle
your
room
Daddy's
boat
COSMO's
room
Daddy's
room
Library
To
the
road
To the
sea
front door
Kitchen
door
Kitchen
Moat
laundry
room
a
Tree
chicken
house
Bird
house
Pond
Animal
house

TWO

★ ★ ★

Esme Unpacks

'It's easy to get lost, so I've drawn a map for you,' Magnus announced, spreading out a scroll of paper and using a small zebra to point out landmarks. 'Here is the yellow corridor. Turn left, take the seventh door on the right and then go all the way up to the top of the turret. Your room is on the left, marked with a cross.'

Then, with the miniature zebra tucked under his arm, Magnus led the way up the stairs from the kitchen with his two brothers in tow. Esme grabbed her case and rushed after them.

After what seemed like a thousand steps, they arrived in a perfectly round white room. 'I picked the flowers. I picked the flowers. I picked the flowers,' said Gus, jumping on the bed as Cosmo kicked him.

'Thanks, Gus. Forget-me-nots are my favourite!' Esme exclaimed, opening the stripey curtains and staring out at the identical turret opposite.

'That's my room,' said Cosmo pointing across. 'I've put a torch under your pillow so that you can flash messages to me if you need anything. I didn't really want to, but Magnus made me do it,' he added, pulling a face.

ESME

'Oh. Well, thanks anyway, Cosmo,' replied Esme, opening her suitcase on the bed to unpack. She went over to a chest of drawers and pulled open the top one. Inside, she found four lizards chasing one another around in a circle. In the next drawer a family of dormice were huddled together dozing in an old pair of knickers. In the next two drawers eggs of various shapes, colours and sizes had been laid out on somebody's jumpers. Esme decided not to disturb them. She opened the wardrobe doors and tipped the contents of her suitcase into the bottom, throwing the case on top and slamming the doors shut.

She hadn't been at all sure what one was supposed to pack for a summer with cousins in a castle full of slightly strange animals, but she had ended up taking:

7 pairs of clean knickers (because her mother had made her)
1 really long rope
2 pairs of jeans
1 tiger print leotard and tutu (for performances)
1 jumper (because her mother had made her)
2 favourite books – Circus Skills and Circus Shoes
1 photograph of her beloved pet, Donk
1 spare sock – (it was all her mother had been able to find but she had promised to send on some new pairs when they arrived in Russia)
1 pair of cowgirl boots
2 pairs of pyjamas that didn't match
4 T-shirts

Now that her unpacking was done, Esme was longing to see the rest of the castle grounds which sat on the shores of a large lake high up on the west coast of Scotland.

'We'll start at the loch,' said Magnus decisively.

Just as they were about to leave the room, Esme heard a strange scuffling sound, followed by faint squawks and muffled pecking noises coming from under the bed.

'What's that noise?' asked Esme, slightly alarmed. 'I think there might be animals under my bed!'

'Don't be silly, Esme,' replied Cosmo dismissively, smiling to himself. 'Hurry up – we haven't got time to be hanging around waiting for you all summer, you know.'

Esme was sure that the squawking sounds were getting louder, but not wanting to be left behind, she chased after the boys down to the beach.

'This is the loch where we keep all the sea animals.' Magnus whistled and the water rippled gently, then four whales, six dolphins, two porpoises and every fish that you could imagine broke through the surface.

The boys waded into the water and Gus clambered onto a nearby porpoise and steered it out to say hello to the whales.

'Come on, Esme,' called Cosmo. 'Just get in! Are you scared or something?'

Esme looked at her cousins, fully dressed in the sea, and waded straight in until she was soaked to her neck. The whales swam up against her legs so that she could stroke them and tiny sea horses bobbed to the surface to gaze at her.

Running her fingers gently through the water, Esme felt the dolphins nuzzle against them as if sniffing her to find out whether she was friendly or not. She ran her hand along their smooth backs and then ducked under the water so that she could say hello nose to nose. The dolphins snuffled her nose and scooped her up for a ride. Esme swirled around in a whirl of happiness with sea horses clinging to her hair. Returning to the shallow waters, she gently tipped the sea horses back into the water and wandered up onto the shore.

Later on, their clothes dried out in the warm sun as they walked along cliffs and through forests, catching rides on giraffes and highland cows before heading back towards the castle.

'We need to start putting the animals to bed,' said Magnus, quickening his pace. 'I will sort out anything larger than a moose. Cosmo, can you tuck in anything smaller than a moose and Esme, can you watch Gus say goodnight to the river creatures?'

The sky was darkening and most of the animals had begun to wander into their enclosures or climb into their trees. Cosmo shooed in warthogs and herded tree kangaroos, curled up alligators and tucked in flamingos' legs, while Esme and Gus wandered over to the river.

Lying flat down on the bank of the stream, Gus sang a jolly lullaby to the river dolphins.

'Little dolphins, dive down deep,
while my lullaby sings you to sleep.
Close your dolphin eyes, don't peep
and I will sing a sleepy song.
Sleep little dolphins, sleep all night,
I would like to hug you tight ...
but you're too rubbery, so I can't.
La la la la la la la.'

Esme leant over the calm surface of the water, whistled a short tune and watched and waited as the minnows came squirling up to see her. Scooping them gently in the palm of her hand, she kissed each of their slippery foreheads, stroked each speckled back with her little finger and slipped the tiny fish back between the watery creases to sleep.

In the quiet of the evening by the stream, Esme realised that this was the first time she had actually left her circus home. It had always travelled with her before, lighting up her evenings with a warm glow of campfires and sequinned costumes.

She was fine without her parents, who were performing most of the time anyway. She could sleep anywhere, having often curled up on top of trapeze stands during their performances, but she suddenly, really quite desperately missed Donk, her pet half-horse-half-donkey.

Esme took a deep breath and clutched Gus's small hand for comfort as they wandered back to the castle. It wasn't until she actually tried to get to sleep without Donk that night that three tears fell from her tired eyes.

'Oh Donk, I can't imagine being anywhere more fun than this. My cousins are great (except perhaps for Cosmo, who is really quite strange), and I don't want to be ungrateful or greedy or ask for anything more, but I want you to know that if I had three wishes now, Donk, they would all be for you.'

Overwhelmed with tiredness, Esme dropped back onto her pillow and quickly fell into a sleepy dream of daring adventures with Donk.

THREE
★ ★ ★
Esme's Surprise

'Esme, wake up! There's a parcel for you!' Esme leapt up as the postal van drove off down the drive. Hooking her feet under her bed she leant far out of her turret window. On the ground below, the boys were examining a strangely-shaped brown paper parcel covered in stamps and tied up with string.

Desperate to see what was going on, Esme jumped out of her bedroom window and turned three perfect somersaults in the air. She landed by the side of the moat.

'Morning,' she said matter-of-factly, as if she had just walked down the stairs.

'Wow,' said Magnus.

Cosmo's mouth hung open in amazement.

'Can I try, can I try, can I try?' shrieked Gus, heading for the turret staircase just as Magnus grabbed his collar and pulled him back.

'It's just circus stuff.' Esme shrugged and smoothed down her pyjama top. 'What's going on?'

At the sound of Esme's voice, the strangely-shaped parcel began to leap about as though something inside was trying to get out. After a few kicks, two hooves appeared through the brown paper packaging and the whole packet came galloping towards Esme, bucking and rearing until a strange head poked out of the paper.

'Wow, that is the ugliest animal Dad has ever sent back!' exclaimed Cosmo. 'I wonder what type of creature it is.'

'Donk!' yelled Esme, flinging her arms around his neck and nuzzling into his slightly

mangy mane. There, she found a label tied to his neck, which read:

Darling Esmerelda,

We were worried that you might be missing Donk, so we have sent him up. He was all mopey without you and wouldn't eat a thing. Hope that you are having a lovely time.

The hunt for new circus acts is going well. We are going to Russia tomorrow to collect some horse jugglers.

Please remember your manners.

All our love,

Mum and Dad

P.S. We will send on socks from Russia

'Magnus, Cosmo and Gus, this is my horse, Donk. Donk, these are my cousins.' Esme made the introductions proudly.

'That is not a horse,' said Cosmo rudely. 'You really don't know anything about animals do you?'

But Esme couldn't care less what Cosmo thought of Donk. Her parents had bought him for her when she was very young and they didn't have much money. Her father had guessed that he was probably largely a donkey rather than a horse, but whatever he was, Esme had been delighted and loved him just the way he was. She had clambered onto his back and ridden him around the circus grounds with great pride, curling up next to him to sleep

in the jewel-lit evenings.

'Ignore Cosmo, Esme. Mrs Larder says that he will grow out of it one day,' said Magnus kindly, shaking Donk's hoof. 'Donk looks like a fine horse to me. Come on, let's go and find him a stable somewhere.'

'Ummm . . .' Esme hesitated. 'Ummmm . . . Do you think that maybe it would be OK if he came and slept in my room? He isn't really used to stables and he might get lonely.'

'No problem,' said Magnus. 'Why don't you take him up?'

Without further ado, Esme climbed onto Donk's back and steered him up the turret stairs by his ears. 'You will love my room, Donk. It's so high up that it's like sleeping at the top of the trapeze stands again – only much quieter!'

They were halfway up the turret stairs when Esme began to hear the same strange

scuffling, hatching and pecking
sounds she had heard
yesterday – except they were
even louder. She leapt off
Donk's back at the top of
the stairs and, leaving
him outside
the door,
she

turned the handle gently and squeezed

inside the room.

Immediately, she found

herself ankle-deep in strange

round baby penguins with fins

down their backs.

Hundreds of them

fluffed around her and as she waded further in, they suddenly started to peck at her. Hoards more were coming out from under her bed. Empty egg shells littered the room. At first the pecking was gentle, but then it started to really hurt and Esme shrieked and battled to squeeze back out of the door. Once outside, she collapsed against it and spat feathers from her mouth.

'Quick, Donk, we have to get help. They can't stay in there. There quite simply isn't enough room!' And without wasting another second, Esme and Donk half-trotted and half-skidded back down the stairs to the kitchen to get help.

FOUR

★ ★ ★

Helter-skeltering Penguins

'Right, we have a problem,' Magnus announced, as Esme jumped from Donk's back straight onto a kitchen chair and sat down.

'How did you know?' asked Esme.

'Oh, I saw Gus trying to catch the puffball penguins that were falling out of your bedroom window. Cosmo seemed to think it would be funny to put hundreds of penguin eggs under your bed to hatch. Dad sent them back from his last trip to the Amazon,' Magnus said, glancing over at a slightly guilty-looking Cosmo.

Meanwhile, Donk snuffled down some teacakes and crumpets from the kitchen

table. After finishing them, he plodded off to the armchair, heaved his hooves over the chair arm and instantly began to snore.

'What's the problem?' asked Cosmo. 'Why not just let them out of the room?'

'What is a puffball penguin, by the way?' asked Esme.

'A puffball penguin is the lesser-known, warm climate, distant cousin of the emperor penguin, and the reason why we can't "*just let them out*" is because their legs are too short to walk down the stairs,' replied Magnus.

'We could roll them,' suggested Cosmo, imagining how much fun it would be to roll a whole load of fat puffy penguins down a spiral staircase.

'We could, except that it's not very kind to the penguins,' Magnus answered, clearing butter and jam out of the way and opening a large dusty book.

Esme and the boys gathered round and peered over Magnus' shoulder to see what he was reading.

Puffball Penguins: a rare breed of penguin, almost extinct in the wild. This small, round variety is easily recognised by their enormous stomachs, extremely short legs and the small dorsal fin running along their backs, thought to be left over from their origins as salmon. Puffball penguins hibernate for ten months of the year, but like to come out and swim in the summer months.

Esme read well although she had never been to school. Her mother thought that school was entirely unnecessary. On the few occasions that Esme had enquired about

going, her mother had replied, 'Life is the best school, Esmerelda. You will learn all you need to know as and when you need it …' And it was true: Esme had.

For example, when she was hungry, she had learnt to eat. When she wanted to catch the circus cat, she had learnt to crawl. When she was longing for candyfloss, she had learnt to ask and when no one had time to help her find out what to feed Donk, she had learnt to read. Ever since she had been able to read, there was nothing that she couldn't learn, although she had struggled to master the unicycle.

Magnus closed the book and the cousins sat back to think, chewing on toast and ideas.

'It's no good; I can't think with that ugly

donkey creature snoring away like a buffalo,' complained Cosmo.

'If they can't walk down the stairs, what can they do?' asked Esme, ignoring his unkind comment about Donk.

'I already said that we should roll them,' replied Cosmo.

Everyone ignored him now and carried on thinking about the problem at hand as Mrs Larder, several rats and a goat trundled in to

clear crumpets and teacakes from the table.

As Esme thought harder, she wondered about high wires and trapezes and whether the penguins could walk on their flippers like seals . . .

'I've got it!' she shouted, jumping up on the table. 'They can slide!'

'Down what?' asked Cosmo, looking at her as though she was completely stupid.

'Down a slide, of course,' replied Esme, looking at Cosmo as though he might not be very clever either. 'We can turn the staircase into a slide and they can slide down it.'

'Excellent idea, Esme,' said Magnus. 'Let's go up to the library and think.'

Esme poked Donk gently in the ribs to wake

him up, wiped teacake crumbs from his whiskery snout, climbed on his back and followed the boys up to the large library in the middle of the castle.

The library was Magnus' favourite room.

He could usually be found here with a creature curled up on his lap and hundreds of books spread out on the floor in front of him. In this vast room, stretching as wide as

his imagination and as far up as his thoughts, Magnus had learnt about how to look after each animal that arrived. He had designed loos for giraffes and studied nest-building for

flying lizards, looked up food for baby parrots and wondered about beds for snakes.

Gus picked up a zebra-striped sausage dog and a copy of his favourite book and sat by the fire whilst Esme, Cosmo and Magnus leapt up library ladders to hunt for information about slides.

'Here,' called Cosmo. '"101 Ways to Build a Slide." This should do.'

Flicking through the pages, they saw straight slides and elephant-shaped slides, bendy slides and upside down slides, bumpy slides and wavy slides, and then on the second to last page they finally found their slide.

FIVE

★ ★ ★

How to Build a Helter-skelter

'That's the one!' shouted Cosmo. 'It's perfect!'

'They can slide round the outside of the turret and whizz off straight to the moat,' said Magnus.

'Can I see, can I see, can I see?' shouted Gus, scrambling over and climbing onto the table to join in the excitement.

Esme read aloud to the others, who made notes. 'Step one . . .'

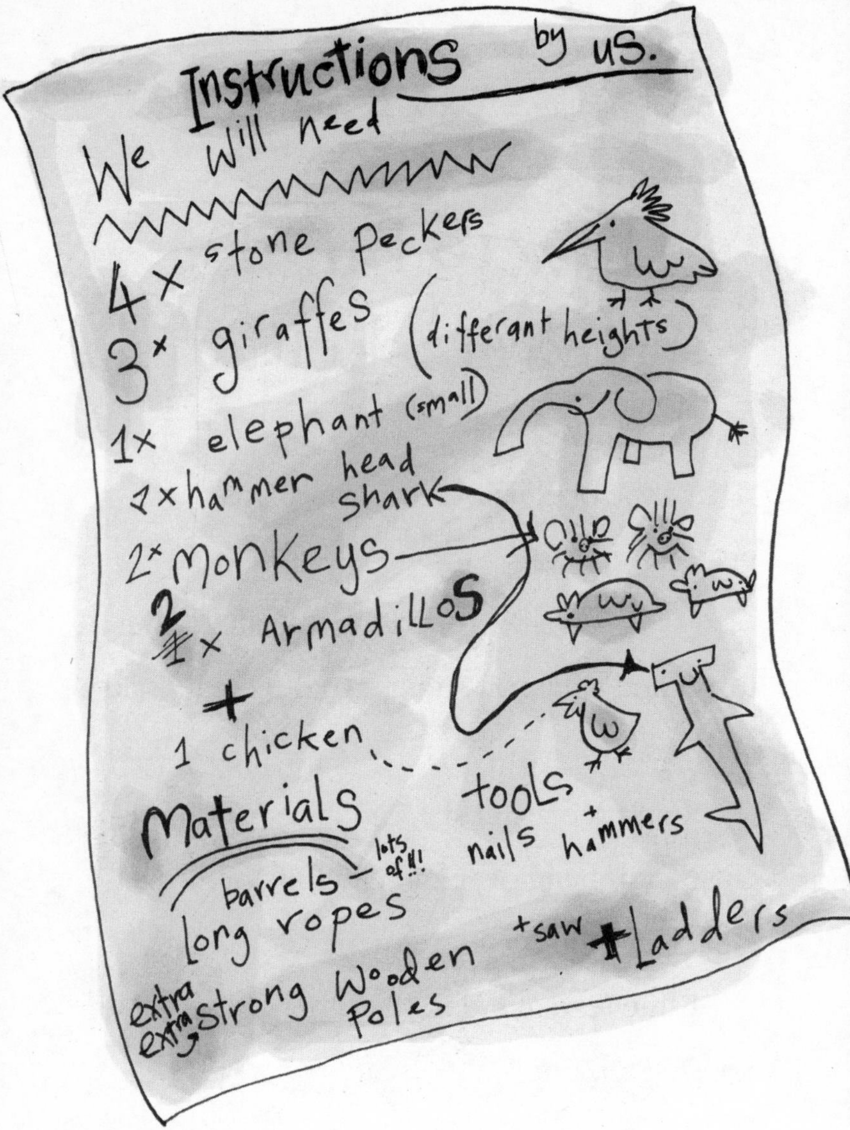

Instructions by us.

We will need

4 × stone peckers

3 × giraffes (differant heights)

1 × elephant (small)

1 × hammer head shark

2 × monkeys

2 × Armadillos

+

1 chicken

Materials

barrels — lots of!!!

long ropes

extra extra strong wooden Poles

tools

nails + hammers

+ saw + Ladders

'Step two,' she continued, 'start at the top and work down.'

Instructions

How to build a Helter Skelter turret slide.

First

old barrel

we need lots!

Saw in half. (ask Mrs Larder to help.)

two halves

‘Step three,’ Esme instructed, ‘when the main part of the slide has been built, rub down

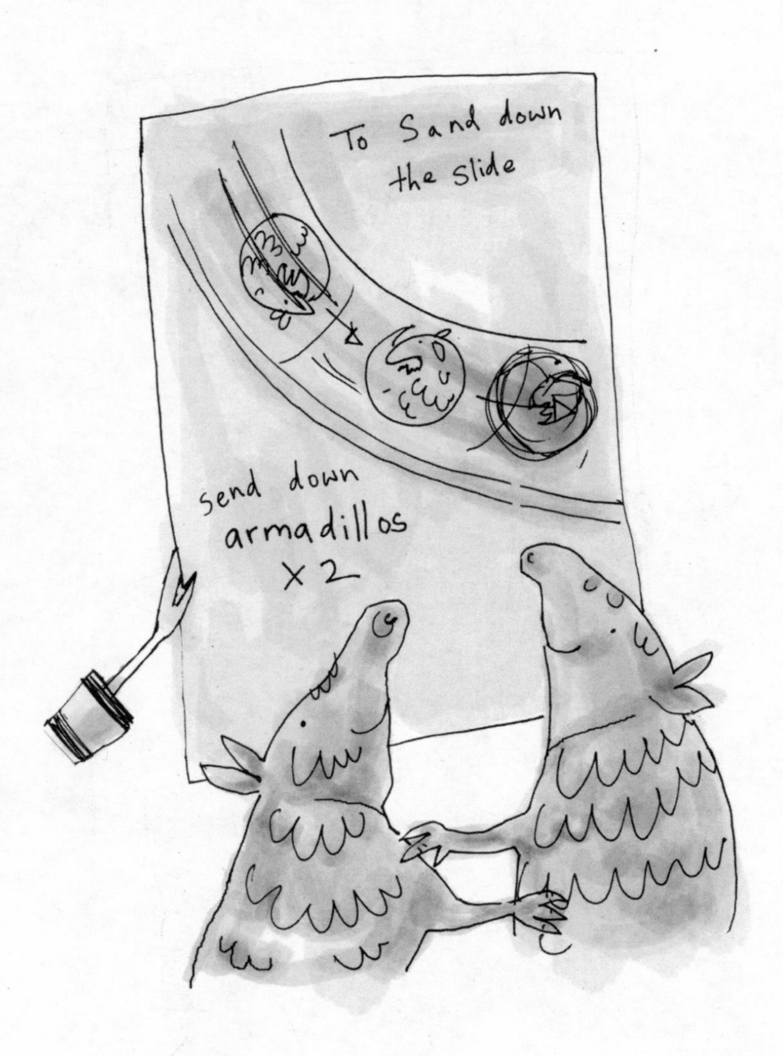

with an armadillo and send down some chickens to check for safety and smoothness.'

Now they knew what to do, the children quickly ran off around the castle grounds grabbing what they needed and herding up animals to come and help. As she was used to heights, Esme climbed nimbly up the

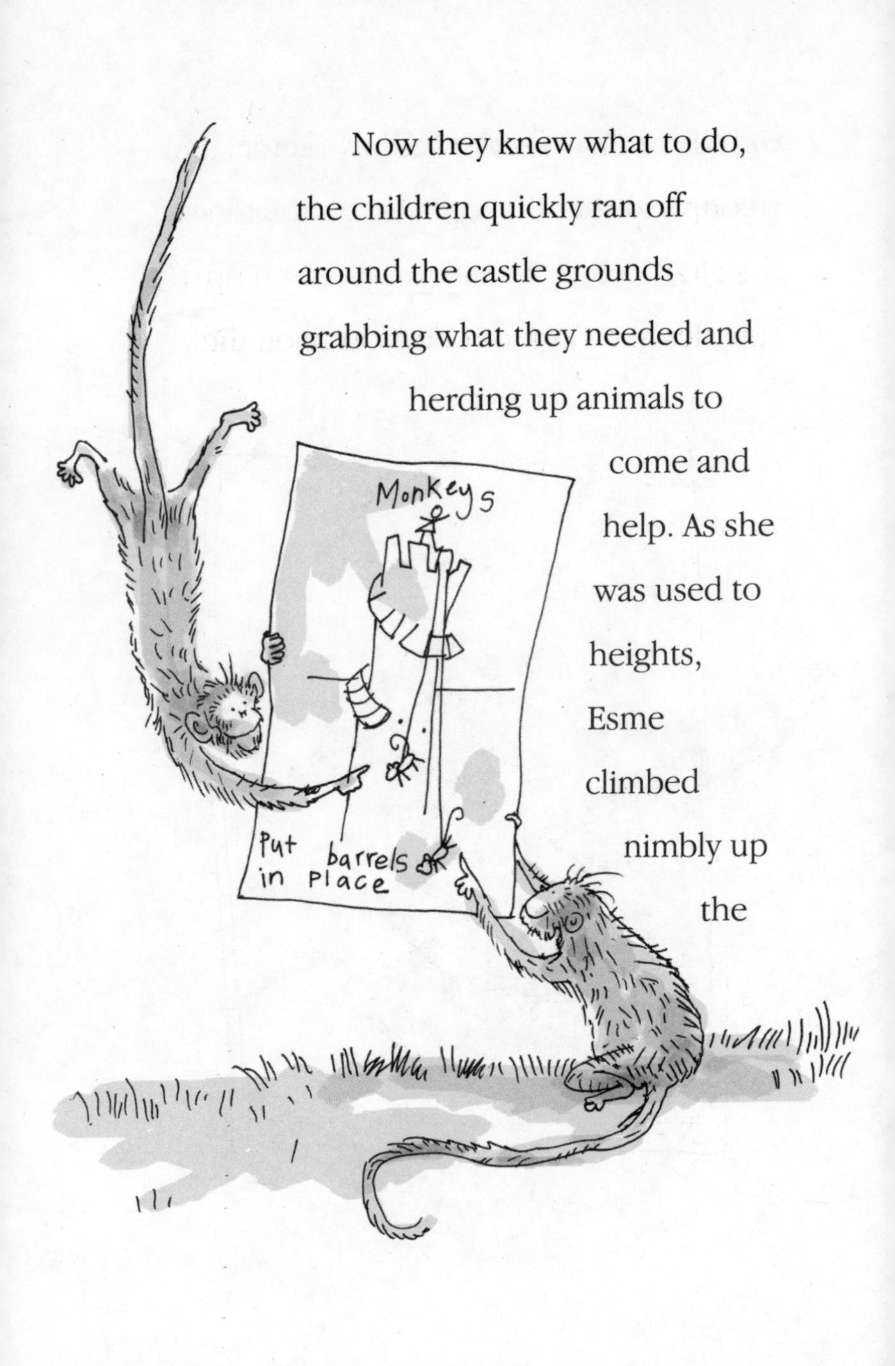

outside of the turret to start work with the woodpeckers at the top. Magnus organised the giraffes and the monkeys to send up supplies and Cosmo rode around on the

elephant with Gus, pretending to be useful.

With much squawking and shouting and sawing and hammering the slide began to take shape.

By the time Mrs Larder sent up a large picnic lunch (which they gobbled hungrily

on the turret roof), the slide already curved halfway down the outside of the turret.

By the time Mrs Larder came up to collect the empty basket and shake the crumbs from the picnic blanket, the slide wrapped twice around the turret and down
to the edge of the moat.

By the time Mrs Larder called for them to wash their hands for supper, the slide wrapped three times around the turret and the children were smoothing down its surface with a couple of rough armadillo shells.

And by the time Mrs Larder had come out of her kitchen to shout at them for not washing their hands, the first chicken shot off the end of the slide and into the moat, almost knocking the housekeeper off
her feet.

Cosmo released the final chicken, watched it swoop around the turret and splash into the water, and then leapt on the slide himself whooping with delight at every bend. He whooshed and whirled, his body twisting high up the sides of the slide as he turned faster and faster around each bend before hurtling with a huge splash into the moat.

'Cosmo, get out this instant! Wash your

hands and run to the kitchen for supper,' shouted Mrs Larder at a beamingly happy but very wet Cosmo. 'And the rest of you had better be there in three and a half minutes or I shall feed your spaghetti to the wolves.' Mrs Larder was not impressed by flying chickens or disobedience.

The cousins were far too delighted with their achievement to mind Mrs Larder being cross with them, but dutifully, one by one, they launched themselves down the helter-skelter and hurried into the castle. They had done it!

SIX

★ ★ ★

The Flying Tigers

Esme wolfed down her spaghetti, spluttering with laughter in between mouthfuls.

'We have to sneak back out after supper,' whispered Cosmo, as Mrs Larder bustled off. 'There is no way I'm waiting until the morning to go on that slide again! Meet in Esme's room. We can fling down the penguins and then play on the slide ourselves.'

As they helped to clear the table, each of the children kissed Mrs Larder's slightly whiskery cheek goodnight and pretended to moan about having to go to bed. Turning the corner out of sight, they pushed one another out of the way, scrabbled up the stairs, then raced along the hall, tripping each other up to get to the top of the turret first.

After shoving penguin after penguin after penguin down the slide, Esme jumped up onto Donk's back as he lay on the top of the slide and stuck out his hooves. Leaning back, Esme's smile was so wide that it almost came off the sides of her face. Racing through the darkness, she and Donk slid dangerously high up the sides at each turn. Esme's wild curls spiralled out behind her as she whipped around the corners, faster and faster until the two of them were fired, sprawling, into the

moat. The splash they made was so enormous that several otters, a couple of penguins and a large salmon were flung onto the banks. Esme quickly returned the startled salmon to the water and watched as it swam off in a hurry.

Then, with enormous splash after

enormous splash, Cosmo, Magnus and Gus followed. They landed one on top of the other and scrambled out to race Esme back up to the top of the turret again and again.

Finally, after at least a hundred turns each, the cousins and Donk all collapsed onto the turret rooftop, exhausted, and stared up at the stars.

'There's the Big Dipper,' announced Esme pointing at a group of stars. 'Alfonso, the tightrope walker, taught me all about the stars and planets. Perhaps we could build one of those next. In the funfair that travelled with the circus there was a big dipper and a big wheel and bumper cars and a helter-skelter like this one, and throw-a-thing-round-a-duck-to-win-a-poor-half-dead-goldfish. I won seven goldfish once but six of them had to be flushed two days later.'

'It must be great to see a circus with a travelling funfair,' said Magnus.

'You must all come and stay sometime. You would love it,' Esme informed them.

'Thanks, Es,' replied Magnus enthusiastically. 'Do you have an act in the circus?'

'Donk and I have a high wire and trapeze act. We're called "The Flying Tigers".'

Cosmo was holding his sides laughing. '"The Flying Tigers"! You'd look more like a pair of flying dodos.' He laughed rudely. 'Only much uglier.'

'One day soon we might actually be

allowed to perform in the circus,' said Esme, ignoring him. 'I can't wait to be good enough. My parents keep saying that we need masses more practice, and then they're always too busy to watch us. Would you like to see our act?' Esme asked eagerly.

'There is no way that weird-looking creature you keep pretending is a horse can even walk straight, never mind fly on a trapeze! Your parents are never going to let you perform!'

'Come on, Donk. Let's get the rope. We probably ought to keep practising anyway,' Esme said, turning away from Cosmo and running to her bedroom desperate to show him he was wrong. Diving into her wardrobe, she peeled her tiger-print tutu from the round tummy of the unicorned pig and rescued her rope from two skipping spider monkeys.

Magnus helped Esme tie the rope to the two flagpoles at the top of the turrets and Donk and Esme climbed on at opposite ends. Esme had squeezed Donk into his tiger-print leotard and he took his position, proudly balancing on one hoof.

'You have to imagine the music,' called

Esme as she and Donk stepped out onto the swaying rope. Donk put one nimble hoof in front of the other, stopping to balance, as Esme did the same on the opposite side. Forwards and backwards they spun, doing

GUS

backflips and side splits and somersaults in mid-air.

Although it had been a little wobbly, when Esme and Donk finished their amazing high wire act with Esme balanced on one leg on Donk's back, even Cosmo was secretly a bit impressed. He made sure his face looked bored though.

'Anyone can do that,' he said dismissively. 'It's easy.'

'Up you get then,' Magnus challenged him.

Cosmo looked up at the rope. Nothing much scared him, but falling from the top of the castle turret was a long way down ...

'Well, what I mean is anyone can do it with a bit of practice. I could do it easily, just not right now,' Cosmo replied a little less confidently.

'The rest of the act is on the trapeze – I can build one between the trees with a bit of help and show you,' said Esme.

'Yes, let's do it soon. That was brilliant.' Magnus scooped up a very sleepy Gus. 'I'm going to put Gus to bed. I'll see you in the morning. Thanks, Esme, that really was great.'

'You are dreaming if you think anyone would actually come to watch that,' said Cosmo nastily as Magnus left. 'Anyway, what use is a circus? Jumping around on a silly rope is all very showy, but it doesn't get anything done does it? Getting us some food would be much more useful – I'm starving. If you're not too scared, you can just jump down to that food shed over there and get us some biscuits.'

'Are we allowed to just take food?' asked Esme.

'Of course, just hurry up and get down there. It's the third hut to the left behind the reptile enclosure. Bring as much as you can.'

Esme peered over the edge of the slide into the darkness. The starlit night had seemed exciting earlier but suddenly it just seemed very, very dark. Esme took a deep breath.

'Quick, Donk, let's go,' she said, far more bravely than she felt.

Around the castle, the blackness became thicker and Esme ran at lightning speed to the wooden hut behind the reptile enclosure.

She grabbed what she hoped was food and stuffed it into a large basket before sprinting back up to Cosmo on the turret roof.

The three of them wolfed down cheese, biscuits, chocolate and apples, then mumbled goodnights to each other and wandered

sleepily back to their bedrooms.

Too tired to wash, Donk licked Esme's face clean as she fell asleep promising to brush her teeth twice in the morning.

SEVEN

★ ★ ★

Mrs Larder is not Happy

Esme and the rest of the house were woken by a furious Mrs Larder stomping around the castle shouting.

'Where has all the food gone?' she yelled. 'I have just asked the bears to dig up all the carrots, bring in the berries and stir the jam, but they are all refusing to work because I don't have any treats for them. And that is because someone or something has been in the food shed and eaten all the supplies! And now I've received a letter from your uncle

saying that he won't be back for another

week! So he can't help either – now what am I supposed to keep the household running on when there's no money for new food and no treats for the animals? The place will fall into rack and ruin in no time and Aubrey trusted me to hold the fort here whilst he was gone. I tell you,' said Mrs Larder shaking her fist, 'I am going to get to the bottom of this . . .'

Mrs Larder threw the note from Uncle Mac down onto the kitchen table.

Esme had never once heard Mrs Larder's really cross voice before and her heart sank as she realised that it was her fault the housekeeper was so very angry. For the first time since she'd arrived at the castle, she wished that her mother was there. She knew her mother would have shouted at her too,

'Esme, how could you be so stupid, trusting that silly boy when he said it was fine to take food? Would you have jumped under a bus if he had told you that was OK too? How many times have I told you to use your own brain?' But at least she knew that her mother would have forgiven her in the end.

She trailed miserably out of the kitchen, her trusty pet by her side.

'Oh, Donk, what if she calls my parents and makes them come and get me? Even with Cosmo getting me into trouble and being rude to you, it's still so much fun here and even though I did take food and eat it, I didn't know that we weren't allowed to and I don't think we could have eaten all of it. That Cosmo!' Esme leant her head on Donk's sturdy back and sighed furiously.

Donk snuffled her kindly and she stroked his comforting velvety snout while she thought about how much she wanted to tie Cosmo up and feed him to an alligator.

'It's OK, Donk,' Esme said eventually. 'Mrs Larder will understand. I will just tell her exactly what happened but I'll try not to get Cosmo into trouble, even though he deserves it. And she will listen and I will say sorry and then it will all be fine.'

Wandering to the top of the stairs in her pyjamas, Esme slid down the banister, almost landing on the still fuming Mrs Larder at the bottom. 'Mrs Larder,' Esme began. 'I am really sorry . . . It was me that took the treats from the shed, but I didn't know that—' Esme

stopped in her tracks as an almost purple Mrs Larder started ranting again.

'Really, Esme, when your uncle agreed to have you this summer, your parents promised that you were a well-behaved girl. Well, taking food without asking is not what I consider good behaviour, and what on earth were you doing wandering around the castle in the middle of the night? And how could you possibly eat so much without being sick? That donkey of yours must have been in on this too. Well, from now on, he will have to sleep in a stable as punishment, and you had better spend time thinking of a way out of this mess or I will have to get in touch with your parents and ask them to come and fetch you!' And with that, Mrs Larder bustled

off, elbows swinging dangerously in all directions.

That was it for Esme. She didn't want to get Cosmo into trouble, but the idea of Donk outside in a stable without her was too much. Esme stormed off to find her cousin.

'Cosmo, you have to tell Mrs Larder that I didn't know I wasn't allowed to take that food!' Esme demanded. 'She's said she might send me home and that Donk has to sleep in a stable.'

'It's not really my fault. You didn't have to listen to me, did you? And it's definitely not my fault that you left the shed door

open

and some of the

animals got in and ate the rest of the treats. That was you being stupid all by yourself,' replied Cosmo, without a care in the world. 'Anyway, if you go home it means more turns on the helter-skelter for me. And besides, that creature of yours belongs in an outhouse where no one can see his ugly face.' Cosmo turned his back on her and carried on play-fighting with a large bear.

Esme thought that perhaps feeding Cosmo to alligators was too kind. But she stopped herself from hitting him really hard in the stomach.

'Arrrghhhhhhhhhhhhgggggggggggggg!' she shouted instead. 'You are the biggest coward I have ever met. You tease me about being scared all the time, but really it's you that's scared. Otherwise you would at least be brave enough to tell Mrs Larder the truth. Ever since I arrived here you have been bossy and mean and I've tried to take no notice, but that's it –

you had better watch out!'

Esme wasn't sure what he was going to need to watch out for, but she did know that she was furious, more furious than she had ever been in her whole life.

No one else could help her. Magnus had gone off to check on the loch animals for the day and Gus was too young to be useful. It was down to her to sort out this mess.

'Right, Donk,' she said when they reached the top of the turret. 'Let's go and have a bath. I think better in the bath.'

As the water ran, Esme and Donk pulled three dozy alligators out of the tub and climbed in between two weasels. The large bath with clawed feet curved comfortingly around the sad girl and the miserable donkey.

Donk stared glumly through the bubbles and watched the weasels in goggles doing lengths up and down the bath. Esme sat at the other end with some paper and a pencil and wrote.

'Hmmmmm,' wondered Esme. 'What did we do at the circus if we needed something?' She sat and thought about the problem for a few minutes. 'I know – we would do a performance and people would pay and then we'd have money and we could buy things,' she thought out loud. She suddenly sat bolt upright. 'That's it! I can do a performance and people can come and use the helter-skelter slide and we can build some more rides and everyone can bring food for tickets instead of money and then I can show Cosmo that people really will come to watch the Flying Tigers!'

Esme began to scribble furiously on her piece of soggy paper.

Esme beamed and poked Donk on the snout with a loofah. 'I have solved the problem, Donk! All we have to do is build more rides and practise our act and then people will come with food. Quick, get out of the bath,' she instructed him. 'We have to go to the library and make a proper plan before Magnus gets back. I don't think I could bear for him to be cross with me too.'

Esme leapt out of the bath and, hardly stopping to dry herself, pulled on her clothes and hurried off to the library with a dripping Donk in tow.

EIGHT

★ ★ ★

Animals and a Circus Fairground

Early that evening, Esme waited at the library window for Magnus to come back. When he did, she explained about Mrs Larder and the lack of food and how Uncle Mac wasn't coming back because of the whale and how she was going to save the castle. Eventually Esme started to feel a little better. She told Magnus that she still had three bars of chocolate left to give to the animals if they would just build the

Magnus

rides, hang the trapeze and be a part of the carousel. He listened thoughtfully to what she had to say and then, when she had finished, he grabbed the megaphone and ran up onto the castle roof.

'Animals!' he called out. 'Just as you all once needed my dad's help, tomorrow we need your help. This is the plan . . .'

Then, as Magnus talked to the huge gathering of rescued creatures below, Esme walked Donk sadly to the stables. 'Don't worry, Donk, I'm sure that the other animals will look after you and make you cosy. And it won't be for long.'

Tucking him under the straw for the night, Esme wished that it was already tomorrow and that they could put their plan into action. Actually doing something would make her feel a whole lot better.

Very soon, hammering and sawing noises could be heard all around the castle grounds.

Everyone bustled around. Mrs Larder, who had been impressed by the children's hard work, had been sewing costumes for hours and now pandas strutted around in sequinned tutus whilst leopards proudly paraded their tortoiseshell leotards.

Magnus was putting the finishing touches to the ghost boat he had designed. Esme was painting, Gus and Donk instructed the animals and Cosmo found as many different ways as he could not to help at all.

Happy but hungry, all the castle inhabitants decorated the grounds in any way they could. The last bright balloon went up and the children ran to the turret and looked down on the fairground circus spread out below. 'I hope someone arrives with some food soon,' grumbled Cosmo.

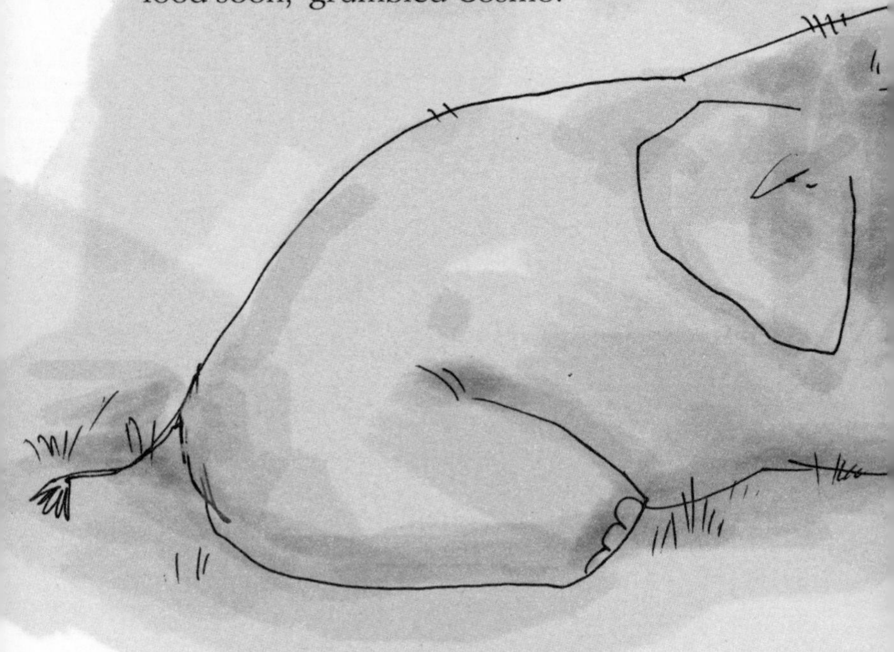

Balloon

NINE

★ ★ ★

The Invitations

'Wow, that's awesome!' Cosmo stood back and stared at the castle and its vast array of amazing rides that the animals and other children had tirelessly built from wood and other spare materials they had found in the castle outhouses.

'Which one shall we try out first?' Magnus said, turning to Esme.

'Can we try the big wheel?' begged Esme.

'Big wheel, big wheel, big wheel!' chanted Gus.

'I'm going on the ghost boat,' said Cosmo. 'Then I don't have to be near *you*,' he added spitefully.

'*You* are not going on anything,' said Magnus firmly. 'You wouldn't help build the rides, so you don't get to go on them.'

'Just try and stop me,' replied Cosmo, marching off towards the ghost boat.

Magnus whistled and a small green rat scuttled over and leapt onto his shoulder. He whispered into its ear and the rat immediately scuttled off.

'I have just asked the water rats not to pull the boat along or to work any of the other rides that Cosmo tries to go on,'

Magnus told Esme. 'It's time he learnt a lesson.' Then, as they reached the big wheel he said, 'I'll go and let the otters know to start paddling and then we can leap on.'

Esme watched in wonder as the giant waterwheel began to turn, slowly at first so that she and Magnus could leap into the seats and pull Gus up with them as they went past. Then, speeding up with each turn, they rose and fell faster and faster. And each time they splashed down into the water at the bottom of the ride, they shrieked more enthusiastically. Soaring up to the top, they rose above woodland treetops and mountain peaks and then watched them disappear as they dropped back down.

When Esme looked down on the castle grounds she saw a tiny Cosmo stomping around crossly, bursting balloons and barging animals out of his way as he went from ride to ride.

'We still have a lot to do,' yelled Esme to Magnus as they whizzed around. 'We have to send out the invitations or no one will know about the fairground circus.'

'OK. Let's go and draw them now,' Magnus called back. Then he whistled to the otters to slow the wheel down. 'I'll meet you in the library,' he said, getting off the ride and heading towards the castle.

Magnus and Esme settled down at the big table and spread out piles of card and pots of glue, felt-tip pens and tubes of glitter. Donk was keeping an eye on Gus outside.

'They need to be really bright so that people notice them,' said Magnus. 'You do some drawings and I'll do the writing and we can see how they look.'

Esme nodded in agreement and the two cousins sat and drew and wrote and drew and wrote and glued until a neat pile of two hundred glittering invitations sat by their side.

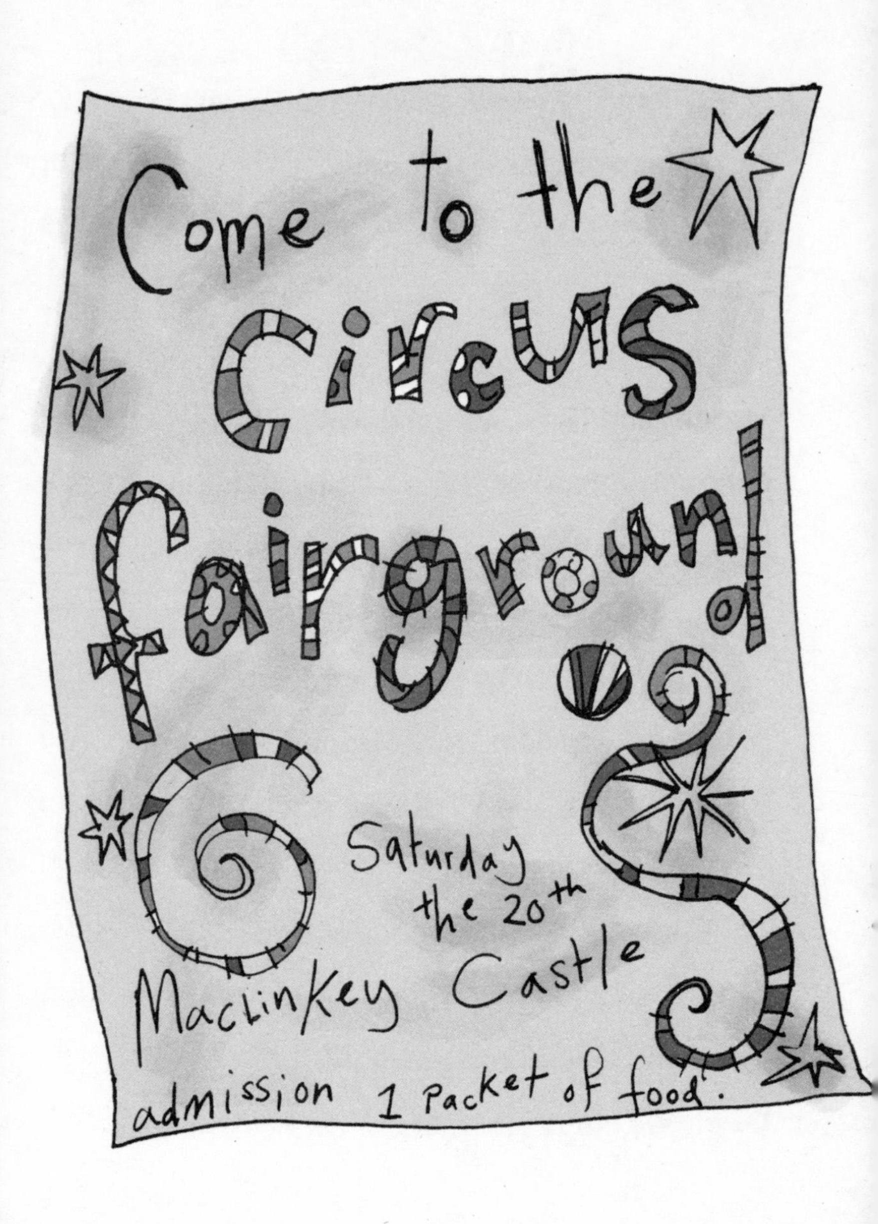
Come to the
Circus
fairground
Saturday
the 20th
MacLinkey Castle
admission 1 Packet of food.

Outside, Cosmo had given up trying to have a go on the rides and was throwing stones at the big wheel. 'Stupid fairground,' he muttered crossly.

'How are we going to get these invitations to the people in the town?' asked Esme when they had finished. 'It's miles away. It would take us a day to walk there and a night to walk back.'

'Birds,' said Magnus. 'They can hold them in their beaks and drop them over the towns. I'm sure they will do us this one last favour . . . is there a tiny weeny bit of chocolate left?'

'I'll run and fetch it,' said Esme.

The birds gathered in the library, perching on the bookcases and the windowsills. Ducks clucked around the feet of vultures and robins sat on flamingos' heads to get a better view. At Magnus' whistle, each of the birds collected an invitation in its beak and flew out through the window.

'No one's going to come and see Esme's silly act anyway. I don't know why you're bothering!' Cosmo yelled as the birds soared and swooped above him to deliver their messages to the nearest town.

But Magnus and Esme didn't care. The sight of their invitations flying high above their heads made them smile. They had done everything they could and now all they had to do was keep their fingers crossed that their plan would work.

Come to the
Circus
fairground

Come to the
Circus
fairground
Come to the
fairground
Come to the
Circus
Circus

Come to the
Circus
fairground!
Saturday
the 20th
MacLinkey Castle
admission 1 packet of food.
Come to the
Circus
fairground!

TEN

★ ★ ★

Esme Miranda's Fairground Circus

As evening silently slid between the mountains, a thousand fireflies settled in front of Maclinkey Castle, outlining it against the dark forest backdrop.

The first few visitors began to crunch up the long pebbled drive to the castle entrance. Gus sat on the gate swapping tickets for parcels of food.

The castle grounds buzzed with excitement. All the rides were in place.

circus
fairground

Welcome t
Candy floss
big wheel
Flying Tigers
incredible diving puff balls

the Circus
ghost boat

The bumper bears were raring to go, the ghost boat was moored in the moat and covered in freshly spun cobwebs and the big wheel had already started to turn.

After forgiving Esme, Mrs Larder had agreed to be the ring master. She strutted around, smartly dressed in a pair of old

fishnet tights and a red riding jacket. She had trained the animals on the carousel to rise up and down perfectly in time with the music as they trotted round in circles.

Visitors climbed aboard the animals' backs and the carousel began. Food poured in and soon popcorn spluttered out from a large pan and a monkey whipped up candyfloss with its tail, clouds of pink puffs floated out into the night before they could be caught.

The fairground circus whirled and whizzed. Laughter and children flew around in all directions as Esme took her place on the highest branch of the tallest tree hanging over the moat of Maclinkey Castle. Her knees were trembling as she straightened out her brightly-sequinned skirt and tucked her curls behind her ears. Down below her, Magnus gathered the crowds by the moat for her performance. She and Donk had practised and practised and practised, desperate to be good enough to perform for a real audience and to prove Cosmo wrong.

'Why did I think this was a good idea?' she whispered to herself shakily. 'Cosmo is probably right – no one will want to see us perform. What if I fall and everyone laughs at me? What if they all get up and leave? I can't do it. I will go to the other tree and tell Donk,' she decided.

Esme turned around and began to climb back down the tree. As her foot reached for a lower branch, she felt something squashy.

'EEEk, EEEk EEEk,' squeaked the ferret she had just trodden on.

Esme looked down and saw a note tied around its neck.

Quickly, Esme read the note: *Sorry. Have told Larder the truth – good luck. Cos. P.S. Flying Tigers are good really*.

Esme couldn't believe it! Beaming, she tucked the note into her skirt and shot back up to the top branch just as Mrs Larder marched out onto the drawbridge cracking a whip she had found under the stairs.

'Good evening, ladies and gentlemen. Welcome to Esme Miranda's Fairground Circus. Let me introduce the star act – the amazing Flying Tiiiiiiiiiiigerrrrrrs!' she roared through her megaphone.

Then, at the final crack of Mrs Larder's whip, Esme leapt from her branch onto her trapeze just as Donk flew in from the

opposite tree to meet her. Her performance had begun. They flew backwards and forwards, turning somersaults in the air as

Flying Tigers

they passed one another. They flew so fast that they became a blur of tiger stripes in front of the audience's eyes.

The first part of the act finished to thunderous applause and great whooping, the crowds stamped and shouted, 'More, more, more!' Esme flipped herself back over to her branch as Donk hooked his hooves over the trapeze. Then he flew out to the middle, let go and did a sideways spin as Esme flew down and grabbed him by the back hooves.

'That's our girl!' Esme heard a cry from the back of the crowd and looked down.

'Mum, Dad!' she yelled, turning a triple somersault before landing.

Two Russian horse jugglers and their four

Shetland ponies ran onto the drawbridge to take her place in the performance as Esme jumped down and ran over to fling her arms around her parents.

'We had no idea that you and Donk were so good!' Her mother glowed with pride and she hugged Esme tightly.

'Thank goodness we made it in time,' said her father warmly. 'We wouldn't have wanted to miss your first performance for all the circus performers in Russia!'

Esme felt as though she might burst with happiness as Donk joined them and she did a little celebratory jig with her beloved pet. Their plan had really worked.

'What the be-gibbons is going on here?' roared a thunderous voice out of the blue.

'DAD!' yelled the three Maclinkey boys, surging towards the loch to greet their father and a giant whale. Esme's heart leapt at the opportunity to finally meet her famous uncle. This was turning out to be the best day of her life!

Dear cousins and Mrs Larder,

Thank you so much for having me to stay
for the summer. I had a great time. Donk is
missing all the other animals and I miss you
all too, but especially the food.

Mum and Dad said that I might be able to
bring the whole circus with me next time, or
you can come and stay here. Donk and I
have started building a caravan because
Mum and Dad have finally agreed to let the
Flying Tigers be one of the real circus acts.
We start next week.

Hope that you are all well. Say hello to the

animals for me and tell the penguins that they can have my room to hibernate in for the winter.

All my love,

Es

xxx

P.S. I left my socks there. Please share them out amongst the animals to keep them warm this winter.

My photo
SCRAPBOOK

By L. Larder (Mrs.)

CIRCUS
MIRANDA
ADMIT ONE

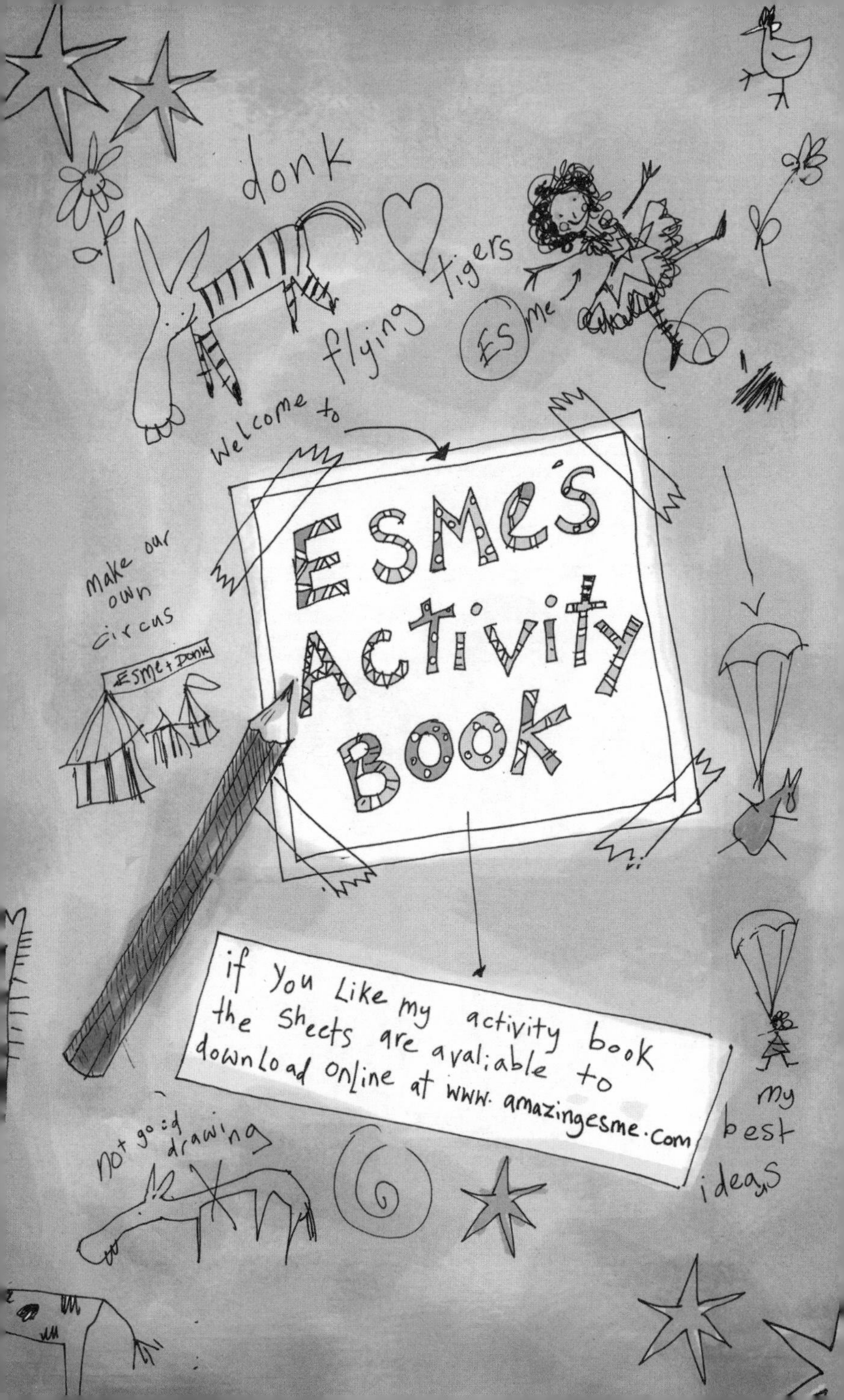

donk

flying tigers

Esme

welcome to

ESME'S ACTIVITY BOOK

make our own circus

Esme + Donk

if You Like my activity book the Sheets are avaliable to download online at www.amazingesme.com

my best ideas

not good drawing

Draw a Map of the Castle grounds

decide where the animals live

Ducks

reptiles

elephants giraffes + chickens

draw your favourite animals

Which Ones would You Like to ride on? (not a chicken!)

Write your own rules for a bad-mannered tea party.

Bad Manners

My Rules by Esme

1. do What you Like!!
2.
3.
4.
5.

Menu

1. chocolate covered cherries
2.
3.
4.
5.
6.
7.
8.
9.
10.

Write your own tea party Menu

draw what you would pack in your suitcase for a Summer away at.....
MacLinkey Castle

Write a Postcard from Esme.

Dear Mummy and daddy,
you'll never guess
what happened when
I got to MacLinkey
Castle..........

Love
Esme xxx
xxx

Send to
Circus
Miranda
Problem: not sure where the
circus is right now.
Solution: send bird!
to find it!

Donk

What might Esme
write on a Postcard
back to her parents?

ENCYCLOPEDIA

imagine some of your own strange animals and write an encyclopedia entry for them.

Draw the outline
of the castle
of the helter
and the skelter
Can you imagine some other
rides that you would build
around the castle?
GLUE
Paint

design some new costumes for Esme and Donk

Can you draw the fairground ride you would most like to have in your garden?

POSTER

Can you design a poster for the circus fairground? What information might you need to put on it?

invitation
Can you think of any other ways that the children could have used to deliver the invitations?
Can you design an invitation for your own circus?

As a child Tamara practically lived in bookshops. She continued her love-affair with reading whilst studying English and Education, specialising in Children's Literature at university.

After a number of years spent as a literacy co-ordinator, Tamara had her first child and decided she would like to live in a children's bookshop again.

As she couldn't find one that she liked, she founded the award-winning *Tales on Moon Lane* bookshop in Herne Hill, filling it with all her favourite books.

One day, she noticed a gap in the shelves in the 5-8 year-old section and, being unable to find many books that she loved, she started to write them herself. That is when *Amazing Esme* turned up!

and the Sweetshop Circus

TANTALISE your taste buds at the Circus of Sweet Treats ...

Join Cosmo and Esme for some
GOOEY WRESTLING

Come, see the magnificent plate-spinning
UNICORNED PIG

Taste heaven-on-a-plate with the
CHOCO-TOFFEE-HONEY-GINGER CRUNCH-SURPREMO ...

... But BEWARE Gus, the crafty lolly-licker

Witness the DEATH-DEFYING high-wire antics of Esme's ANIMAL ALLSORTS

Thanks for coming!